Daddy's Rainbow

CW00793295

WITHDRAWN FROM STOCK
WITHDRAWN FROM STOCK

2843 783

For Erin,
and in memory of her wonderful daddy, Ben
– L.R. xx

For anyone who has lost someone special.
– B.C.

BLOOMSBURY CHILDREN'S BOOKS
Bloomsbury Publishing Plc
50 Bedford Square, London, WC1B 3DP, UK
29 Earlsfort Terrace, Dublin 2, Ireland

BLOOMSBURY, BLOOMSBURY CHILDREN'S BOOKS
and the Diana logo are trademarks of Bloomsbury Publishing Plc

First published in Great Britain 2022 by Bloomsbury Publishing Plc

Text copyright © Lucy Rowland 2022
Illustrations copyright © Becky Cameron 2022

Lucy Rowland and Becky Cameron have asserted their rights under the Copyright, Designs and Patents Act, 1988,
to be identified as the Author and Illustrator of this work

All rights reserved. No part of this publication may be reproduced or transmitted in any form or by any means, electronic or mechanical,
including photocopying, recording, or any information storage or retrieval system, without prior permission in writing from the publishers

A catalogue record for this book is available from the British Library

ISBN 978 1 5266 1577 0 (HB); ISBN 978 1 5266 1578 7 (PB); ISBN 978 1 5266 1579 4 (eBook)
10 9 8 7 6 5 4 3 2 1

Printed and bound in China by Leo Paper Products, Heshan, Guangdong

MIX
Paper from responsible sources
FSC
www.fsc.org
FSC® C020056

To find out more about our authors and books visit www.bloomsbury.com and sign up for our newsletters

Lucy Rowland

Daddy's Rainbow

Illustrated by **Becky Cameron**

BLOOMSBURY
CHILDREN'S BOOKS
LONDON OXFORD NEW YORK NEW DELHI SYDNEY

Erin's Daddy saw colour in everything.
Even on grey days when rain pitter-pattered.
When drops danced and drizzled down
window panes, Erin's Daddy would say,

"Up you get and off we go!"

They'd pull on yellow wellies for puddle jumping
and Daddy would tell Erin,

"We can't see rainbows without the rain."

On spring days Erin and Mummy
helped Daddy in the garden.

"Look at all these weeds!"
said Erin's Mummy.

"Weeds are flowers too,"
smiled Daddy,

"if you look at them the right way."

Summer days with Daddy needed sunglasses,
with blue so bright it shone!

In autumn, their walks
were full of crunchy red,
scrunchy orange and
shiny conker-brown.

At night they saw these
colours too, when they
warmed their fingers
by the fire.

Winter days were
sometimes white.

"They're like blank pages in a book," Daddy said.
"And it's our job to fill them with colour."

At night when dark was all around,
Daddy showed Erin how black is beautiful.
He told her,

"Stars can't shine without the dark."

But slowly things began to change.
Erin found that winning races with Daddy was getting easier.

The flowers in the garden
didn't seem so bright
anymore.

Rainy days were just wet and cold again.

Mummy explained that Daddy was very poorly.

Later there were hospital visits,
hushed voices and held hands.

There were cuddles,
closed doors and then . . .

Quiet.

And everything turned grey.

Erin missed Daddy and his magic.
Mummy missed Daddy too.
They missed his laugh and his cuddles.

They missed his silly singing in the car
and the voices he did at story time.

Erin missed the way that Daddy made pancakes with funny faces on! She missed his colours.

It was then that Erin remembered the scrapbook.

She showed it to Mummy.

Mummy began to laugh at the pictures.
Erin laughed too. Soon their faces started to look smiley.

The next day Mummy said,

"Up you get and off we go!"

She pulled her yellow wellies on and told
Erin stories about puddle-jumping
in the rain.

She told Erin stories
about crunchy leaves,

snowball fights

and planting seeds.

She told Erin stories
about Daddy.

By then, the rain had almost stopped,
though not completely.

And as they walked back home again, they both saw . . .

Daddy's rainbow.